Published by Ladybird Books Ltd
A Penguin Company
Penguin Books Ltd, 80 Strand, London WC2R 0RL, England
Penguin Books Australia Ltd, 250 Camberwell Road, Camberwell, Victoria 3124, Australia
Penguin Group (NZ), cnr Rosedale and Airborne Roads, Albany, Auckland, New Zealand

Meg and Mog Television Series copyright © Absolutely/Happy Life/Varga 2003
Based upon the books featuring the characters Meg and Mog
by Helen Nicoll and Jan Pieńkowski
Licensed by Target Entertainment
This book based on the TV episode **Mog in Charge**
Script by Carl Gorham and Moray Hunter
Animation artwork by Roger Mainwood
First published by Ladybird Books 2005
2 4 6 8 10 9 7 5 3
Copyright © Absolutely/Happy Life/Varga, 2005

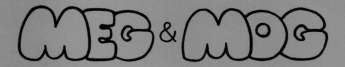

Mog in Charge

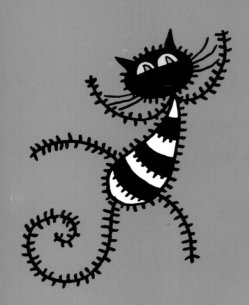

created by
Helen Nicoll and Jan Pieńkowski

Meg, Mog and Owl were having breakfast. Mog was in a bad mood.

"Today," said Meg, "I'd like to visit the Witches."

"I'd like to visit the Owls," said Owl.

Mog sighed very loudly.

"I'd like to visit the Witches and **then** the Owls," said Meg.

"I want to visit the Owls and **then** the Witches," said Owl.

Mog shouted, "Does anyone want to know what I want?"

"Sorry, Mog," said Meg. "What do you want?"

Mog waved his arms. "I want to be in charge!" he said.

Meg and Owl looked worried.

"OK," said Meg. "You can decide what we should do."

"Hurray!" shouted Mog. "Today we are going to . . ." he thought hard, "eat my favourite food."

Mog whispered something to Meg.

"Are you sure, Mog?" she said.
"I'm in charge!" said Mog.
So Meg stirred the cauldron.

"Fish and fish
  And fish and – fish,
  Make us all
  A fishy dish."

At first nothing much happened.
Then the cauldron began to rattle
and shake. "Here we go!" cried
Mog, holding out a plate. A tiny
fish popped out of the top of the
cauldron.

"That's not much for three of us,"
said Meg.

But the cauldron continued to rattle
and a larger fish jumped out.
"That's better," said Mog.

The cauldron kept on rattling. More fish leapt out of its mouth and soon the plate was full.

The fish were getting bigger and bigger. Before long the floor was covered with fish.

Sea water began to pour out of the cauldron.

"Oh dear," said Meg. "This is worse than one of my spells."

An octopus, some dolphins and a whale swam out. The water was rising fast and was already up to Mog's waist.

"Help!" shrieked Mog.

A small boat floated out of the
cauldron.

"Quick, get in the boat!" said Meg.

Mog suddenly remembered
something. "Hey, wait a minute!
I'm in charge."

"Oh sorry, Mog," said Meg. "What
 shall we do?"

"Quick, get in the boat!" yelled Mog.

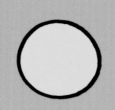

Meg, Mog and Owl drifted along
on a calm sea.

"It's not that bad," said Mog.

Owl spotted a dark shape in the water.

"SHARK!"

"Oh no, it **is** that bad!" cried Mog.

Shark fins appeared on every side and surrounded the boat.

Meg and Mog grabbed an oar
each and rowed as hard as they
could. Owl flapped along above
them, shouting encouragement.
"Aim for that island!"

Gasping for breath, Meg and Mog
propelled the boat on to the beach.
The sharks snapped their teeth, but
it was too late. Meg, Mog and Owl
were safe.

"Phew!" said Mog.

"What a wonderful island," said Owl.

It was a jungle paradise.

"Look at those birds," said Meg.

"And look at those flowers," said Owl.

"I give in," said Mog. "I don't want to
  be in charge any more."

"Shall I do a spell?" asked Meg.

"Yes please, Meg," said Mog.

"Ear of frog
  And wing of bat,
  Save us from
  This big wild cat!"

There was the huge flash of light and a small furry bundle dropped into Meg's arms.

"You've turned him into a baby tiger!" said Mog.

"Well done, Meg," said Owl.

After they had taken the baby tiger
back into the jungle, Meg said, "So
what would you two like for tea?"

"You decide, Meg," said Mog.
"You're in charge now – thank
goodness."

"Hear, hear," said Owl.